On the Boardwalk

by Thomas Hischak

Single copies of plays are sold for reading purposes only. The copying or duplicating of a play, or any part of play, by hand or by any other process, is an infringement of the copyright. Such infringement will be vigorously prosecuted.

Baker's Plays
7611 Sunset Blvd.
Los Angeles, CA 90042
bakersplays.com

CHARACTERS

(4 women, 5 men)

MR. SANFORD STAUNCH – a New York City banker

JACK STAUNCH – his son, a captain in the military

MRS. MALAPROP – a rich widow

LILY FLETCHER – her niece, in love with Jack

FARLEY DANES – a poet

JULIE WHITAKER – Lily's friend, in love with Farley

SHAMUS O'SLUGGER – an Irish boxer

WILLY FURROW – a farmer with money

LOUISE – Lily's maid

SETTING

On the boardwalk of Atlantic City

TIME

Summer of 1910

AUTHOR'S NOTES

The setting remains the same throughout the play. A section of the boardwalk, perhaps raised a bit above the floor, runs across the width of the stage. There are two wooden benches on the boardwalk. The view behind it can be that of the ocean with some of the sandy beach or the audience can be facing the shops and restaurant along the boardwalk. All entrances and exits are made left or right where the boardwalk continues. After the prologue, the action takes place all in one day so each character has only one costume, except Jack who later dons a military uniform.

PROLOGUE

(All nine characters are posed across the boardwalk and are frozen in silhouette. LOUISE steps off the boardwalk into the light and addresses the audience. Perhaps music plays under the entire prologue.)

LOUISE. I don't know where you folks was during the summer of 1910 but I was in Atlantic City where I had a very profitable summer helping the course of true love. And I'm not talking about just one pair of turtle doves, oh no, but a whole flock of them! You see, I was working as a lady's maid for Miss Lily Fletcher and we was spending the summer at this hotel on the board-walk. Well, we were there no more than a week before romance struck. There was this fella –

(JACK comes to life and crosses down to LOUISE in the light.)

JACK. Louise! I've got another letter for you to deliver!

LOUISE. Oh, Captain! Or should I say…Mr. Pippin?

JACK. That's the idea, my girl. Here. *(gives her the letter)* See that Miss Fletcher gets this without her aunt seeing you.

LOUISE. Don't I always? I'll slip it to Miss Lily the second the old dragon turns her back. But how come you sign all your letters Jonathan Pippin? Miss Lily would like you just the same if she knew you was really Captain Jack Staunch.

JACK. It's a subterfuge, Louise.

LOUISE. A what?

JACK. So that Mrs. Malaprop cannot discover my true identity.

LOUISE. I don't know nothing about no subterfuge but I'll deliver the letter all the same.

JACK. *(slips her a coin)* That's my girl. Ever since I met Miss Fletcher on the Boardwalk last week my world has been turned upside down.

LOUISE. Yes, that happens sometimes, sir.

JACK. And ever since then the Boardwalk has become my favorite avenue!

(He returns to his original position and freezes in silhouette.)

LOUISE. As I was saying, once Miss Lilly and that Captain Staunch set eyes on each other it was all hearts and flowers. Of course it weren't going to be so easy with Miss Lily's aunt always on the lookout. But I managed pretty well to –

*(**LILY** breaks her pose and joins **LOUISE** in the light.)*

LILY. Tell me, Louise! Has a letter come for me?

LOUISE. It sure has, Miss Lily. Here. *(gives her the letter)*

LILY. Oh, Louise! From my Jonathan?

LOUISE. That's right. But you better read it fast. Your aunt has a way of just poppin' up –

*(**MRS. MALAPROP** breaks her pose and joins them in the light. **LILY** hides the letter.)*

MALAPROP. Ah, here you are, Lily! Out in the morning sun without your parasol! My niece, are you not aware of the manner in which the sun can percolate your delicate skin? Go inside at once before you are quite overcome with heat prosperity.

LILY. Yes, auntie. *(returns to her original position and freezes)*

MALAPROP. Goodness, I have tried to the best of my agility to raise my niece to be an educated girl who knows fine manners and the ways of social predicate. But sometimes I get so disparaged when I see the result.

LOUISE. She seems okay to me.

MALAPROP. You couldn't possibly understand, Louise. You haven't the approximate breeding. *(looks around to be sure **LILY** is gone)* I have another letter for you to deliver, Louise.

LOUISE. For that boxing bloke with the funny way of talking?

MALAPROP. Mr. Shamus O'Slugger is not a "boxing bloke," Louise. He is a gentleman plagiarist from Ireland and is quite emerged in high society, seen only at the best of places.

LOUISE. Sure. I seen him in a saloon brawl just the other night.

MALAPROP. Tell him it is from his beloved Delilah who awaits his response with the greatest expectoration.

LOUISE. I'll tell him. But have you ever met this Irish scamp?

MALAPROP. Of course not. We have not been properly introduced. But I have seen him from afar, Louise, and he appears to me to be the very pineapple of manliness!

LOUISE. Whatever you say, Mrs. Malaprop. *(takes the letter)* If you like Irish stew –

MALAPROP. And Louise… *(pulls out a coin)* A little something extra for your inconveyance.

LOUISE. Thanks. *(takes coin)* Something extra is always welcome, even if it's little.

(**MALAPROP** *returns to her original position and freezes.*)

LOUISE. Who woulda thought the old girl had a romantic streak in her? Well, I guess Atlantic City in summer can do that to a gal. Now this Irish bloke she has set her cap on –

(**SHAMUS O'SLUGGER** *breaks his pose and crosses down to near* **LOUISE** *in the light. He wears boxing gloves and spars with an invisible partner.*)

SHAMUS. There! That'll teach you to lower your left! *(sees* **LOUISE***)* Ah, my darling postal angel! Is it another letter from my beloved Delilah that you be bringing me?

LOUISE. It sure is, Mr. O'Slugger. Here. *(gives him the letter which he immediately reads)*

SHAMUS. Faith, bless you, child!

LOUISE. Now I know this Delilah is a secret admirer and all but haven't you ever wondered who she is and what she looks like?

SHAMUS. Oh, but the secret is out. I saw you with herself yesterday and I must say I was overwhelmed.

LOUISE. That's a good word for it.

SHAMUS. You were on the Boardwalk with that frightful old gorgon…then *she* came out of the shop and joined the two of you. Ah, what a piece of poetry she is!

LOUISE. Uh huh…

SHAMUS. So don't try to be coy with me, my girl. I've seen her and, apart from her excellent good taste in men, she is a wonder to behold! *(showing the letter)* And how she writes! Such words I never knew back in the old country! I am thinking, the young thing must be inspired by me! There's no other way to put it!

LOUISE. I won't put it no other way then.

SHAMUS. I'll have a response for her presently. Don't go away!

LOUISE. I'll stick around if you make it worth the wait.

SHAMUS. Certainly, my little post mistress!

*(**SHAMUS** return to his original spot and poses in a boxing position.)*

LOUISE. That piece of Irish stew is sure gonna be disappointed once he realizes who Delilah really is. But in the meantime I hope to make a bit of a profit from both of them. Speaking of letters, there was some heart-tugging mail going on that summer between Miss Lily's friend Julie Whitaker and this moody young poet fellow named Farley Danes. But them two used the U. S. Post Office so I didn't get no part of that action.

*(**FARLEY DANES** and **JULIE WHITAKER** break their poses and cross down to far left and far right where they read their letters to each other in two spotlights.)*

JULIE. My dear Mr. Danes, I will be joining my friend Lily and her aunt in Atlantic City for the July Fourth holiday. How pleasant it will be to see the ocean again and walk the very boards where first we met last summer.

FARLEY. My dearest and devoted Julie, the three weeks since last I've seen you last have been endless in their tedium and Promethean torture! But the very thought that this separation will someday end has given me the strength to actually take food and water on occasion.

JULIE. I am glad to hear it. Perhaps, Mr. Danes, you will be able to spend the holiday by the sea as well. I know of one to whom it will bring a very pleasant satisfaction.

FARLEY. And I can think of one tormented soul who will feel nothing short of ecstatic rapture at the prospect! I will be there, my divine one!

JULIE. *(to audience)* How pleasing it is to be loved by a poet!

(**JULIE** *and* **FARLEY** *return to their original positions and freeze.*)

LOUISE. Oh, and there was another visitor to Atlantic City that summer. Willy Furrow was this farmer who —

(**WILLY FURROW** *breaks his pose and crosses down to* **LOUISE** *with a letter.*)

WILLY. Just the gal I need to see. Louise, ain't it?

LOUISE. That's what they still call me.

WILLY. You remember me, don't you? Pricklepear Farm, last May during the cherry blossom season?

LOUISE. Oh sure, I remember you, Mr. Furrow! You was the one that taught Miss Lily how to ride side saddle.

WILLY. You got it! Willy Furrow's the name and riding is my game! I got more acres and more horses than I got hay in my hair, and that's no joke! *(laughs)*

LOUISE. What are you doin' here in Atlantic City? Ain't no horse racing on the beach, is there?

WILLY. Gads and geldings!! Nothing like that. It's love, my girl! True and everlastin' love!

LOUISE. You don't mean – ?

WILLY. When I heard from my friend Captain Staunch that Lily Fletcher was going to be here for the Fourth of July doin's, I said to myself: William, my boy, clean up your boots, put on your city duds, head to the ocean and propose to that gal before another breedin' season goes by. So here I am!

LOUISE. Well, Miss Lily sure will be surprised to see you, Mr. Furrow.

WILLY. That's what I thought. So I wrote this here letter to her to sort of break the ice. It says why I've come and all, to kinda get her in the right frame of mind. Then I seen you! Bridles and broncos!! Do you ever deliver personal letters?

LOUISE. On very rare occasions.

WILLY. *(pulls out a bill)* Oh, I'm make it worth your bother. Here. *(gives her letter and bill)* You are now carrying a declaration of love! Pretty excitin', ain't it?

LOUISE. I'll say so. Don't you worry, Mr. Furrow. I am Cupid's messenger. And for this kind of money I'll take flying lessons!

WILLY. Dobbins and donkeys!! I am in the City of True Love! *(returns to his original pose and freezes)*

LOUISE. So you see what I mean when I says there was a whole flock of love birds in Atlantic City that summer. If only I could keep everything and everyone straight –

*(**SHAMUS** breaks his pose and returns to **LOUISE** with a new letter.)*

SHAMUS. Here you go, my darling. Let you be delivering this to my sweet Delilah and don't be surprised if she blushes something powerful. I've got words in there that will sweep the dear girl off her feet!

LOUISE. I'm sure she's never gotten a letter like this one before.

SHAMUS. And a little something for Cupid's messenger. *(gives her a coin)* Make haste!

LOUISE. I'll be sprouting wings any minute now!

(**SHAMUS** *returns to his original position and freezes.*)

Some folks just don't trust the mail, especially when love is in the air. And I can't says I blame them. Anything can go wrong with postal letters or telegrams and such. That's what I'm here for. I can take care of all that and come out with some profit of my own. And if you don't believe that, you just keep watching.

(**LOUISE** *returns to her original position and strikes a pose in silhouette as the music ends and the lights black out.*)

End of Prologue

ACT ONE

*(**LILY** sits on a bench reading. **LOUISE** enters with a basket.)*

LOUISE. I've tramped up and down this boardwalk, Miss Lily, and I can't find you one copy of *Romance in Ragtime!*

LILY. How about *The Long Island Love Nest* or *The Lady From Trenton?*

LOUISE. Nope! Looks like everybody in Atlantic City is reading the same stuff this summer.

LILY. And here I am stuck with the sermons of Dr. Humphrey Clinker! My aunt's idea of holiday reading!

LOUISE. I did see a copy of *The Exploits of Lilly Langtry* in one book shop but the picture on the cover was so sensational I was too embarrassed to pick it up.

LILY. What did you get then?

LOUISE. Look at this. *(taking books out of her basket) The Fatal Connection.* It sounds like a humdinger. *The Gordian Knot. Cape May Intrigue.* And this one: *The Memoirs of a Lady of Quality Written By Herself.*

LILY. *(taking the books)* I suppose they will have to do. But I did have my heart set on *Romance in Ragtime.* My friend Julie told me all about it and I blushed just listening to her.

LOUISE. Oh oh. I see your aunt coming!

LILY. Quick! Into the basket! *(stuffing books into basket)*

LOUISE. And she's got some old gentleman with her.

LILY. Now where did Clinker's sermons go?

LOUISE. Here it is!

*(**LILY** pretends to read the book as **MRS. MALAPROP** enters with **MR. STAUNCH**.)*

MALAPROP. There she sits, Mr. Staunch, a girl of incomprehendable deception!

LILY. Good morning, aunt.

MALAPROP. To look at her you would never suspect the pretty thing of such duplexity!

STAUNCH. Not to look at her, madam. She is quite the loveliest of girls.

MALAPROP. Do not be hoodwacked by her, Mr. Staunch. She has given her affections to a scoundrel named Jonathan Pippin, a nonemnity I have never met who is as full of mystery as he is of secretion. I was fortunate to contracept one of his letters to her and discovered the whole affair on my own recompense.

STAUNCH. Shocking! Yet I must admit she is so very appealing to the eye –

MALAPROP. My niece, do you know who this gentleman is?

LILY. I regret I have not yet made your acquaintance, dear sir. *(goes to him, takes his hand and smiles)*

STAUNCH. By heavens, charming as well!

MALAPROP. Charm is an obituary thing, Mr. Staunch. *(to* **LILY***)* This gentleman is Mr. Staunch from New York City. He is very promiscuous in the banking industry.

LILY. Pleased to meet you, Mr. Staunch.

STAUNCH. As am I, my dear girl!

MALAPROP. He is also the father of Captain John Staunch, the man I have chosen to be your perspective husband.

LILY. Husband? *(laughs)* Auntie, no one does prearranged marriages anymore. Young people decide these things for themselves.

MALAPROP. I am your aunt and your guardian and I will decide for you! Further discussion is incumbent! Louise, take my niece back to the hotel.

LILY. I willingly go. But I must tell you that nothing in the world could ever induce me to give up my beloved Jonathan!

MALAPROP. Louise!

LOUISE. Okay, okay. Come along, Miss Lily. I got that new book of moral essays in my basket here and I know how you been itching to read it. *(exits with* **LILY***)*

STAUNCH. I'll admit she does have a streak of stubbornness in her.

MALAPROP. A streak? She is undulating with it! And after I have been so careful to raise her with the most uterus care. You see, Mr. Staunch, I believe a girl brought up with fine manners and a thoroughbred education will prove a credit to her sex and genus.

STAUNCH. Fine manners, of course, Mrs. Malaprop. But I believe educating a pretty young girl is asking for trouble. I notice she likes to read books. A dangerous sign, I say.

MALAPROP. Books selected by myself, Mr. Staunch, and guaranteed to improve the mind and simulate the intellect. Education is a supercilious thing when properly sublimated and directed by a knowledgeable person. I consider myself a highly capacious guide, particularly when it comes to the art of speech.

STAUNCH. Is that so, madam?

MALAPROP. Isn't it oblivious? Oh, the joy one can get with good learning! The rewards of reading cannot be denied. I myself have read the great classics, from the plight of that poor King Oedifice and the ovulations of Cicero to the studies of Mendel who taught plants how to be inbred. I have studied maps in order to learn about the contagious nations and have turned the globe in order to memorize its different fractions. And what has it taught me? The beauty of words and grammar, Mr. Staunch. The glory of the English language and all its subsidiaries. And this I will continue to do every day so that I continue to border my horizons!

STAUNCH. Madam, you leave me speechless!

MALAPROP. A condition you will never find me in, Mr. Staunch. Come. Let us go and and seek out your son. I am very anxious to make his acquiescence.

STAUNCH. But the young lady seemed so adamant –

MALAPROP. Do not worry about Lily. She will soon see the error of her ways. I have a plan that will abbreviate her affections for this rascal Jonathan Pippin. Then she will go and besmirch your son for his hand.

STAUNCH. Your niece is such a divinely beautiful creature that I am sure everything will work out in the end.

MALAPROP. It will, Mr. Staunch. It will. Your son, with his noble character and family disposition, and my Lily, with her fine education and pleasing physical attrition, will wed and live together among the wealthy genitalia!

(*MALAPROP and* STAUNCH *exit together as* JACK *and* FARLEY *enter from the opposite side.*)

FARLEY. But you have not told her your true identity yet?

JACK. I haven't. Not because I wish to continue deceiving Lily but because I so love how much she loves this Jonathan Pippin!

FARLEY. But *you* are Jonathan Pippin!

JACK. Exactly! When we met on the Boardwalk and she asked my name I didn't have the heart to say Jack Staunch. "Staunch? The New York City Staunches?" she'd have to ask. "The banking Staunches with their millions and –" Oh! And there she sat so lovely and bright and I said to myself: Jack, this is the genuine article. But will she love you for yourself? I couldn't risk it. So I told her I was Jonathan Pippin, a penniless artist with nothing to call my own but myself.

FARLEY. And her aunt disapproves of this Pippin as a suitable match for her niece?

JACK. Absolutely! And it makes Lily love me all the more!

FARLEY. Well, you will have to tell both of them the truth eventually.

JACK. Of course. But in good time, dear Farley. In good time.

FARLEY. I wish I had your patience. I have been sick with anticipation concerning Julie…er, Miss Whitaker.

JACK. But why? She loves you, doesn't she? There are no obstacles to your loving her, are there? What do you have to worry about?

FARLEY. The whole world is a threat to our happiness! When we are separated I can only imagine the most disastrous things happening. If it is sunny I worry that she might be too exposed to the sun and faint. If it rains I am obsessed that she might catch a chill. When there is no letter from her I fear she has hurt her hand or has stopped loving me or has forgotten me completely or – !

JACK. *(laughs)* Steady, my good man! I know you poets look at life with a more sensitive eye than us prosaic types do; but can't you enjoy your love?

FARLEY. Enjoy it? What kind of love would that be? The torment my worrying brings me is the one proof I have that it is true love.

JACK. Have you seen Julie yet?

FARLEY. No. I have only just arrived and the hotel clerk said she had gone out shopping. Oh, I pray that she is well and still loves me!

JACK. *(laughs)* How can she not, my dear Farley! You are worth more laughs than a pair of Dutch comics!

FARLEY. Do not mock me, Jack. I am not so thick-skinned as yourself.

JACK. Ah! Here comes someone who can set your mind at rest!

FARLEY. Is it her?

JACK. Not quite. I see William Furrow coming down the Boardwalk. You know good old Willy, don't you?

FARLEY. I don't think so.

JACK. He lives less than a mile from your Julie. He has a ridiculously large horse farm, Pricklepear Farm it's called, and Lily took some riding lessons with Willy when she was visiting Julie last spring. Oh, you'll like Willy. He's a bit of a poet himself.

(**WILLY** *enters in gentlemanly summer clothes that do not seem very comfortable on him.*)

WILLY. Is it Jack? My old pal Jack Staunch? Gads and geldings!! It's great to see you again, Jack!

JACK. William, my favorite country bumpkin! Got most of the hay out of your hair, I see! (*Both laugh.*)

WILLY. I tried! Dobbins and donkeys!! I didn't expect to find anyone I knew in Atlantic City! Not my usual turf.

JACK. I should say not. What brings you to the sea? Come to make fun of the swells?

WILLY. Oh, Jack! I'm not the gawking type! I come on a mission of love!

JACK. Love? Found a horse that you're just aching to buy?

WILLY. Oh, she's a filly, all right! But a girl!

JACK. You sly old clodhopper! I thought you only cared about four-legged beauties! Let me introduce you to my friend from New York. Farley Danes, this is William Furrow. I made Willy's acquaintance at the race track. Farley here is a poet and a lover. I met him at college and he has proved to be an education in himself!

WILLY. Glad to know you, I'm sure! (*shakes hands*) You caught me on a day when my hands are clean!

FARLEY. Pleased to meet you, Mr. Furrow. I understand you know Miss Julie Whitaker?

WILLY. Little Julie? Ever since she was shin high! You can practically spit from her house to my breeding field!

JACK. You hear that, Farley?

FARLEY. How convenient. Have you seen Miss Whitaker of late?

WILLY. Let's see. When's the last time I set eyes on little Julie? Oh! It was a week ago last Saturday. That was it! At the Lumbly's barbecue.

FARLEY. At a barbecue? And was she in good health?

WILLY. Julie? Healthy as an ox and as rarin' as a bullock!

FARLEY. I beg your pardon?

JACK. She's well, Farley. Not sick at all!

FARLEY. Oh. I see.

JACK. Well, don't sound so disappointed.

FARLEY. Oh. Wonderful. I am pleased to hear it. And, Mr. Furrow, did she seem…okay?

WILLY. Bridles and broncos!! Julie was fine!

FARLEY. Fine?

JACK. Willy, you yokel, Farley here is in love with Julie Whitaker! Can't you give him any more details than "fine"?

WILLY. You're Julie's sweetheart? Well, why didn't you say so! Let's see. When I last saw her she was bloomin' with good health and cheer. Why, at the barbecue she looked as pretty as a photograph, her eyes sparkling and her laughter enough to make the sun shine.

FARLEY. She was laughing?

WILLY. Laughin' out loud to beat the band!

JACK. You hear that, Farley? She was laughing!

FARLEY. But I don't understand? What was she laughing about?

WILLY. She don't need a reason! The girl was happy!

JACK. You hear that, Farley? She's happy?

FARLEY. Well, yes, I'm pleased that she is – What has she to be happy about? We have been separated from each other and have not set eyes on the other since – !

JACK. Farley! She's in love. Isn't that reason enough?

FARLEY. Oh. I suppose so.

JACK. What else, Willy?

WILLY. Well, I remember while we were waiting for the grub a bunch of folk sat themselves on the lawn and Miss Julie started singin' like a lark welcomin' the dawn – !

FARLEY. She was singing?

WILLY. Singin' as loud as a brass band!

JACK. You hear that, Farley? She was singing!

FARLEY. Why would she be singing? Was she sad? Were they sad songs?

WILLY. Not at all! Bright and cheerful ditties all 'round!

FARLEY. It makes no sense. Why sing then?

WILLY. For the benefit of the crowd, I tell you!

FARLEY. For the crowd! What need has she to entertain the public?

JACK. Because she is happy, Farley! And a girl who is in love and so happy would quite naturally join in if everyone else was singing.

FARLEY. Oh. I guess that is quite natural. Under the circumstances.

JACK. What then, Willy?

WILLY. After the vittles was all ate up, the moon climbed up high and folks' feet was itchin' so they kicked up their heels and started dancing. And there was Miss Julie just like some feather tossin' in the breeze – !

FARLEY. She was dancing?

WILLY. Dancin' to outdo the whole band!!

JACK. You hear that, Farley? She was dancing!

WILLY. In five counties there just ain't no one can dance quite like that girl!

FARLEY. That is enough! Laughing is understandable. To be happy is to laugh. And singing – well, one cannot help singing upon occasion. But dancing! How could one even consider dancing when separated from one's beloved? It is inexcusable! Why, Jack, have you seen me laugh of late?

JACK. Not for years, Farley old boy.

FARLEY. Or singing? It is in my nature to sing? On any occasion?

JACK. No. Not on any occasion.

FARLEY. There you have it. And as for dancing –

WILLY. But she looked so happy!

JACK. You hear that, Farley? The girl is happy!

FARLEY. This is intolerable! *(exits in frustration)*

WILLY. Did I say somethin' wrong, Jack?

JACK. *(laughs)* Not at all, Willy! It's just that we're dealing here with a man in love.

WILLY. Which reminds me! I got some courtin' of my own to do. I better skedaddle!

JACK. But you haven't told me all about this filly that has stolen your heart away.

WILLY. Not now, Jack. I've got to find the hotel she's boarded at. Talk to you later!

(Starts to exit as **STAUNCH** *enters, and* **WILLY** *bumps into the old man.)*

Whoa there! Get off the track if you can't hold the inside curve!

STAUNCH. I beg your pardon!

WILLY. *(to* **JACK***)* Talk about your swells…! Good day, Jack! *(exits laughing)*

STAUNCH. The foolish oaf! Is that the sort you pal around with, Jack?

JACK. Father! What brings you to Atlantic City? Not pleasure, is it?

STAUNCH. Business of sorts.

JACK. Of course. The bank.

STAUNCH. Not this time, Jack. My business is my spendthrift son whose commission in the Army hardly begins to cover his expenses.

JACK. Oh, that. Old business.

STAUNCH. Yes. Same old story. But instead of a lecture I have news for you.

JACK. I shall miss the lecture. But go on.

STAUNCH. I have decided to settle your affairs once and for all. You will be given the house on Murray Hill, the property in Hyde Park, a generous amount of funds – too generous, I might add – and your independence. You will be free of me and will become your own man. God bless you or the devil take you – it's up to you.

JACK. Father, I don't know what to say…

STAUNCH. Just don't say anything insolent. I'm at an age
  when I want peace and quiet in my family. I'm not getting any younger or healthier. So accept my offer and
  let's shake on it.

JACK. *(shaking his hand)* Of course I accept. Haven't I always
  been a dutiful son?

STAUNCH. Well…more or less.

JACK. I shall try to be more than ever. Do you wish me to
  give up my commission in the Army?

STAUNCH. Oh, that will be up to your wife, I suppose.

JACK. My wife? *(laughs)* Father, you might recall that I am a
  bachelor!

STAUNCH. You don't have to remind me! A disgrace, at
  your age, to be living for pleasure. Well, marriage will
  put a stop to that. The lady will see to it.

JACK. Lady? What lady?

STAUNCH. Your wife! Aren't you paying attention?

JACK. You mentioned houses and money and freedom –
  nothing about a wife.

STAUNCH. I didn't? Well, a wife comes with the settlement.
  And a very good match, I must admit.

JACK. I cannot believe my ears! You have selected a wife for
  me?

STAUNCH. Of course! You don't think I'd trust anything so
  important to you? No. The lady comes with the deal.
  You buy the farm, you get the livestock in residence.

JACK. Livestock! That certainly speaks volumes about the
  sort of woman you have chosen for me!

STAUNCH. Don't you worry about her. I know what I'm
  doing.

JACK. I can just imagine. Some ugly old dowager dripping
  in stocks and bonds with five cats in her Long Island
  estate – !

STAUNCH. I tell you the woman will be as old and as ugly
  as I choose! She may be cross-eyed and have a hump
  on her shoulder as well! You will wed her nonetheless!

JACK. Thank you for your kind offer, Father, but I fear I must refuse the houses and the money and the charming matron and your good company forever!

STAUNCH. You are in no position to refuse! What will you live on?

JACK. On my commission and the knowledge that I will never have to communicate with you again! Good day, sir. I hope you enjoy the rest of your stay in Atlantic City. *(exits)*

STAUNCH. *(shouting after him)* I won't stay a minute longer if there be any chance of running into you! I don't want to breathe any of the air that you have already tasted! I refuse to inhabit the same hemisphere with such an ungrateful son! *(to self)* If he were a farm I'd foreclose on the insolent cur!

(STAUNCH exits the opposite way, passing LOUISE who is coming down the Boardwalk.)

LOUISE. Was that Mr. Staunch? He's looking more like his name than ever! And him with all that money. What good is it if you go around looking like an angry prune? *(sits at bench, pulls out a small notebook and pencil)* Now let's see…to bring the accounts up to date. Two bits from the Captain for delivering his letter from Jonathan Pippin. Ten cents from Miss Lily for acceptance of the same letter. Half a dollar from the boxing bloke for delivering his letter to Delilah. A nickel from the old dragon for accepting it and delivering one back to him. A person could starve being in her confidence! Then one dollar from the horse fellow for his letter to Miss Lily. At such prices I wish more farmers would use my service. Then two more bits from the Captain for a new letter this morning which I delivered instead to the old lady and made a whopping fifteen cents for my deception. But my conscience is clear. She already knew of the affair and the letter was just fuel for the fire. You'd think that such a double cross would be worth more than fifteen cents! That makes a total of…two dollars and thirty cents since the day before last! And the holiday is far from over! *(puts away her book and rises)* Oh, what would the lower classes do if the upper classes weren't so foolish?

*(**SHAMUS** enters.)*

SHAMUS. There's the little darlin'! Is it shadow boxing you've been up to, lass?

LOUISE. I don't think so, Mr. O'Slugger.

SHAMUS. I've been looking for you up and down the Boardwalk but you seem to disappear with each move I make.

LOUISE. I been kinda all over the place, if that's what you mean.

SHAMUS. But now I've found you and something tells me old Irish heart that it was worth the wait. Have you not a little thing for me, my girl?

LOUISE. I got a letter. I hope that's what you mean.

SHAMUS. From my Delilah!

LOUISE. It ain't from Uncle Sam. Here. *(gives him the letter)*

SHAMUS. Rapture! That is the only word for it, dear child. Rapture! *(reads)* "My beloved Shamus…!" Such a pretty hand! *(continues reading to self)*

LOUISE. Oh, her hands are just about perfect. Both of them.

SHAMUS. Listen to this: "Female punctuation forbids me to trust my infinitesimal affection to ink but if you can read between the lines the pretext will say all…!" Faith, your lady is the mistress of language! She is the very queen of the dictionary!

LOUISE. Well, Mr. O'Slugger, a woman of her experience –

SHAMUS. Experience! Why, what experience can one have at her young age?

LOUISE. I mean…She sure reads a lot! Book after book after book. It sure is something how she reads!

SHAMUS. And speaks so? Does she ever talk about me in your presence?

LOUISE. Oh, all the time! It's Shamus this and Shamus that and Shamus morning noon and night! When she's not reading, that is.

SHAMUS. Further rapture! *(takes out coins)* Take this, my sweet – ! What is your name?

LOUISE. Louise.

SHAMUS. My darlin' Louise! *(gives her coins)* Here's something to buy yourself a little treat on the Boardwalk. And take this… *(kisses her hand)* It will put you in mind of my appreciation.

LOUISE. Oh, Mr. O'Slugger! What would my mistress say if she knew you was so friendly to me?

SHAMUS. She will know I am a man great of heart and full of passion! If she asks you, tell her I kissed you fifty times!

LOUISE. Oh, but that would be lying.

SHAMUS. Nonsense! *(kisses her on cheek)* There. *(kisses her on other cheek)* And there. *(kisses her on lips)* And there again! A little later I will have a new letter for you to deliver and, in time, I will bring the total up to fifty.

LOUISE. Letters?

SHAMUS. If necessary. *(kisses her again)* But I mean to save you from lying.

(Both have been enjoying the kissing and he tries again but **LOUISE** *moves away.)*

LOUISE. My goodness! I thought you boxing blokes were only interested in one thing.

SHAMUS. And what might that be, Louise? *(gets close)*

LOUISE. Boxing.

SHAMUS. Pshaw! The game is more complex than you think. The thrill of the sport! Well, I'm thinking there are various kinds of thrills. Underneath this bold and brawny Blarney Stone of a man hides a gentle lover. My heart is gigantic and my affection can be as forthright as me fists!

LOUISE. I must remember that.

SHAMUS. And remember this, my darlin' Louise. *(kisses her one more time)* Adieu! *(exits)*

LOUISE. If I didn't know better, I could take a fancy to that big hunk of Irish stew. *(writing in her book)* "Thirty cents from Shamus O'Slugger for...letter delivery and kisses."

*(**JACK** enters, muttering to himself.)*

JACK. Trying to marry me off to one of his rich old ladies just to keep her money in his bank...!

LOUISE. Captain!

JACK. How could he think I'd fall for such a ploy?

LOUISE. I don't know. How could he?

JACK. But I'll never give in to the old buzzard – !

LOUISE. Captain, I got good news for you and I got bad news. Which one you want to hear first?

JACK. Things could not possibly get worse. Tell me the bad news.

LOUISE. All right. That last letter you wrote – I mean, that Jonathan Pippin wrote to Miss Lily...

JACK. Yes? What of it?

LOUISE. Well, I'm afraid Mrs. Malaprop got a hold of it. It wasn't all my fault, Captain! I was real careful but – !

JACK. It doesn't matter, Louise. She was bound to find out sooner or later. And with my father's latest folly it looks like Jonathan Pippin is to die soon in any case. I must see Lily right away – *(starts to exit)*

LOUISE. But, Captain! Don't you want to hear the good news?

JACK. What? Oh. Of course. What is it, Louise?

LOUISE. Your father is making arrangements for you to marry –

JACK. *(in agony)* Oh! Don't say it!

LOUISE. To marry Miss Lily!

JACK. What's that?

LOUISE. I heard it myself. Mrs. Malaprop and the old man told Lily she was to marry his son John or else!

JACK. John? That's me! So Lily is the fat old matron!

(Overjoyed, he embraces **LOUISE,** *picking her up off the ground.)*

Louise, you are an angel!

LOUISE. Captain! Miss Lily ain't fat or old!

JACK. I know! Isn't it marvelous! *(pulls out coins)* Here you go, Louise!

LOUISE. You want me to deliver another letter?

JACK. No. That's for not telling Lily that I am John Staunch. Not yet, at least. Do you understand me?

LOUISE. I guess so. But if you marry that girl she's gonna find out you ain't no Jonathan Pippin when the preacher asks "Do you – ?"

JACK. I know! But until then you must promise –

LOUISE. Okay. But my goodness! You sure don't like to do things the easy way, do you, Captain?

JACK. *(laughs)* I suppose not, Louise!

LOUISE. I got to be going now. *(to self)* No way that Miss Lily is old or fat…! *(exits)*

JACK. My very own Lily…! And intended for me all along! Oh, father, there might yet be some wisdom in that old addlebrained head of yours! But I think Jonathan Pippin cannot be gotten rid of. Not yet, in any case.

*(***STAUNCH*** enters grumbling to himself.)*

STAUNCH. The impudence of the boy! I'll disown him and then cut him off without a penny. And then live another fifty years just to spite him!

JACK. Father…?

STAUNCH. Out of my way, fellow! I'll have nothing to do with you! *(starts to leave)*

JACK. It is understandable, dear sir. Such a disappointment I must be to you.

STAUNCH. Disappointment? You're a damnable pain in my abdomen!

JACK. I will not remain in your sight if it distresses you. I only wish to admit my past foolishness and annoy you no further. Good day. *(starts to leave)*

STAUNCH. Foolishness! That's one word for it! Wait, Jack! What are you saying?

JACK. Only that I have reflected on what you last said to me and realize how correct a father can be. But my presence upsets you so I will depart –

STAUNCH. Jack! What is this? Come back here!

JACK. I obey. As I should in all things.

STAUNCH. Now that sounds more like a son of mine! In all things, you say?

JACK. In all things of importance.

STAUNCH. Now you're talking, my boy! And marriage?

JACK. What can be more important than marriage?

STAUNCH. I have a son again!

JACK. I just hope that it is not too late to accept the woman you have wisely selected for me.

STAUNCH. Too late? Not at all! Just in time! And wait until I tell you about her, Jack! Oh, your heart will leap and you will sing out with joy!

JACK. Don't worry about my heart; it exists only to please you, father. As for singing, I am joyful just to make you happy.

STAUNCH. Of course, of course. But listen to me. A young Miss Lily Fletcher is holidaying here in Atlantic City with her matron aunt. Oh, wait until you see her! Such perfection! Her eyes! Her smile! Her –

JACK. Which am I to marry? The young lady or the aunt?

STAUNCH. The aunt? Jack, what's the matter with you! I'm offering you the loveliest, most – !

JACK. Because it makes little difference to me. You know best about these things –

STAUNCH. Jack, my boy, come to your senses!

JACK. I have, Father. And I will obey you in all things.

STAUNCH. Good God, Jack, listen to me! Perfect! She's perfect!

JACK. Perfect, Father? Whatever pleases you pleases me.

STAUNCH. And charming! She has a smile that could charm the birds out of the tree!

JACK. It's no matter how she smiles as long as she pleases you.

STAUNCH. And her face! As fresh and pure as milk! And graceful! She flutters like some butterfly!

JACK. If that's the sort of thing you like.

STAUNCH. And so lovely! You won't find a girl quite so young and fair!

JACK. Let her be old, dear sir, or plain, if you prefer. I am ready to wed anyone you choose.

STAUNCH. And there there are her eyes! Bright and sparkling!

JACK. Who cares? I suppose she has two?

STAUNCH. What is the matter with the boy! Is he made out of clay! *(to* JACK*)* Do you hear what I am saying? The lady is perfect! Wait until you meet her. And if you don't fall instantly in love I...I...I will marry the girl myself! Come along!

JACK. I will obey.

*(*STAUNCH *exits then* JACK *follows laughing.* FARLEY *enters alone. A waltz is heard coming from a player piano in the distance.)*

FARLEY. So she laughed. What harm is there in that? And sang on occasion. That seems only natural. And as for dancing – ! Oh, that is a damned insistent little tune. I wish it would stop. But wait – ! Could it be? That is the same tune that was playing on the day I first set eyes on Julie. On this very Boardwalk! The same music! The same place!

*(*JULIE *enters.)*

And the same lady! *(goes to her)* How pleasant to see you again, Miss Whitaker.

JULIE. Very pleasant, Mr. Danes.

FARLEY. May I say you are looking well and seem to be enjoying the best of health?

JULIE. You may say it, Mr. Danes, but I was not so well as I am now that you are here.

FARLEY. Oh, Julie! Then you do still love me, I hope?

JULIE. Your hopes are confirmed, Farley! I do.

FARLEY. Then, despite your behavior, all is well!

JULIE. Despite what behavior, Farley?

FARLEY. It is nothing. I will not think on it any more!

JULIE. You will not think on what? I don't understand you.

FARLEY. Well, you know a fellow named Furrow? William Furrow? He comes from your county.

JULIE. Indeed, I know Willy Furrow. But what has he to do with – ?

FARLEY. Nothing at all, really! It's just that he was telling me about some barbecue you attended and the silly farmer was exaggerating madly about how you – Oh, I cannot even recall what he said now.

JULIE. Please try to recall it, Mr. Danes. I am growing very curious.

FARLEY. So what if you were laughing? Can't a girl laugh if she is happy? And as for singing, well, it's most understandable. And then the dancing – I suppose that could be explained somehow.

JULIE. I do not feel the need to explain anything, Mr. Danes!

FARLEY. And there is no need that you should, Miss Whitaker. I have put the whole business out of my head.

JULIE. How gallant of you, sir, to excuse what you imagine to be my outrageous behavior! I hope someday to be able to return the compliment!

FARLEY. Do not be angry, Miss Whitaker. All is forgiven!

(The music offstage stops.)

JULIE. Forgiven? Now I see, Mr. Danes, that you question my loyalty and devotion!

FARLEY. Not at all! But if your love for me was indeed serious –

JULIE. Serious! Like yours, I suppose?

FARLEY. Well…yes. Like mine. I was not the one dancing. I was too miserable to dance. My heart was so full of love that I could not even consider such a thing!

JULIE. So you measure the sincerity of one's affection by the degree of misery one experiences?

FARLEY. Is there any other accurate measure?

JULIE. Well, Mr. Danes, I see that I have been a great disappointment to you. I apologize for not being in abject pain and so I will remove myself from your sight and never bother you again with my good health and lack of ostentatious misery. *(exits)*

FARLEY. Such a feckless and inconstant woman! How could I have believed her love was anything more than a mere distraction? *(starts to go, stops)* What have I done!

*(**FARLEY** rushes off in the opposite direction from **JULIE** as **JACK** enters with **MR. STAUNCH**. **JACK** now wears a military uniform.)*

STAUNCH. Now I want you to be a credit to your uniform and behave like any other healthy American male when you meet Miss Fletcher: fall helplessly in love with the creature!

JACK. As you wish, Father. My only wish is to please you –

STAUNCH. Stop with all that! It's enough to make a man ill!

JACK. Yes, sir.

STAUNCH. Ah! Here comes Mrs. Malaprop now. And a damned interesting woman she is too, even though I can't understand her half the time.

*(**MRS. MALAPROP** enters.)*

MALAPROP. And this, I may consume, is Captain Staunch! So pleased to meet you at last. You have been highly accommodated to me by your dear father.

JACK. And let me say, Mrs. Malaprop, that even though I have not yet met your niece, I am very favorably inclined to the arrangement because of the honor of being related to yourself. You are a woman of such learning and manners that when the name of Mrs. Malaprop is brought up, no tongue is silent.

MALAPROP. *(to* **STAUNCH***)* Such fine manners he has, Mr. Staunch! You did not tell me John was so fallible. I quite approve of him.

STAUNCH. He has his moments, Mrs. Malaprop. But what is the latest with your niece? Has she come around yet to accepting my Jack's hand in marriage?

MALAPROP. The ignorant child still insists that she loves this dyslectic Jonathan Pippin, a man whom none of us has seen and nobody knows anything about. Even when I presented your preposition of matrimony she stubbornly claimed to love this penniless artist!

JACK. I will not take offense at such behavior, Mrs. Malaprop. I am sure she will soon see her way to acknowledging your superior judgment.

MALAPROP. You are very patient to take such an aptitude, Captain. The girl is very stubborn and I fear this Pippin scoundrel has filled her head with the some reptilian ideas. Listen to this… *(pulls out a letter)*

STAUNCH. What is that, Mrs. Malaprop?

MALAPROP. A letter from the rubicon written to my niece. Luckily I was able to approximate the correspondence before my maid had a chance to present it to Lily.

JACK. *(nervously)* A letter from Jonathan Pippin, you say?

MALAPROP. The very personification himself! Read it, Captain, and you will see for yourself what kind of vivacity he communicates to her.

JACK. You wish me to see a letter intended for Miss Fletcher?

STAUNCH. Read it, my boy! You heard the lady!

JACK. As you wish. *(reads)* "My dearest Lily, idol of my soul. How I wish it were my own ready lips, rather than my words, now being touched by your fingertips." *(to* **MALAPROP** *and* **STAUNCH***)* Very prettily phrased, don't you think?

MALAPROP. Outrageous! To mention fingertips to an unmarried lady!

STAUNCH. He sounds like a damn fool to me. What next?

JACK. *(reads)* "Since your last letter, oh! what anguish I have suffered since I learned about him. I am referring, of course, to him, my feeble rival."

MALAPROP. That is you, Captain!

STAUNCH. Feeble, indeed! No one calls my son feeble!

JACK. "But more than the blunderings of this Captain Staunch, I fear the trouble a certain matron may cause us. That weather-beaten she-dragon with a face like a –" *(to* **MALAPROP** *and* **STAUNCH***)* What is he talking about?

MALAPROP. Me, sir! He means my very personage!

STAUNCH. The impudent little puppy!

JACK. "But let the old crow keep a watchful eye. We shall outwit her with our plans even as she continues the massacre of the English tongue."

MALAPROP. There! Did you hear that? An attack upon my language!

STAUNCH. It's inexcusable! I'll take a strap to the boy!

MALAPROP. It is an aspersion on my parts of speech! To be accused of such a thing! I, who use words as carefully as the surgeon uses his scapular!

STAUNCH. The brute! Leave me with the cad for five minutes and I'll teach him a thing or two!

MALAPROP. But there is worse to come. Read on, Captain.

JACK. "But let the old crow keep –"

MALAPROP. You need not read that part again, sir. The next section, if you please…

JACK. "But never you fear the old harpy. Our mutual happiness is long overdue! Soon you will be forever free of the cunning old –"

MALAPROP. You may skip to the end, if you don't mind.

JACK. Certainly. *(reads)* "Before long, Lily, we'll speak face to face, then I will tell you my intricate plan for our happiness together. I remain your own, Jonathan Pippin."

MALAPROP. Did you ever hear of such an odorous thing? He thinks he can outwit me! Me! The very epilogue of watchfulness!

STAUNCH. The foolish boy doesn't know what he's up against, Mrs. Malaprop. That's very clear.

MALAPROP. At least I can gain some gravitation knowing that my niece never received this letter and has not read the scandalous condiments it contains.

JACK. We all can be grateful for that, Mrs. Malaprop.

MALAPROP. But I see her coming this way now. I told her to meet me on the Boardwalk at precisely one o'clock and here she comes at one-oh-twelve. Is that not indigenous of youth today?

STAUNCH. Shameful! Now prepare yourself, Jack. She is a charming girl for all her stubbornness!

JACK. Perhaps the lady will be more susceptible to my presence if she were to first meet me alone. Should the two of you retreat into one of the shops and I was to introduce myself to her, we might have much more success in the matter.

STAUNCH. Capital idea! What do you say, dear lady?

MALAPROP. If you think it adventitious, Captain. I am willing to try any method to help exfoliate this Pippin fellow from her mind.

STAUNCH. Come with me, Mrs. Malaprop. We will sample the salt water taffy in that candy shop over there.

MALAPROP. I don't usually divulge in sweets, Mr. Staunch, but in your case I will make an exertion. Good speed to you, Captain!

(She and **STAUNCH** *exit.)*

JACK. Do I tell her the truth now? Oh, to look on her again! I cannot risk her refusing me. The charade must continue a little longer, I think.

*(***LILY*** enters.)*

LILY. Jonathan! What is the meaning of this costume? Are you going to a masquerade?

JACK. You are not far from the truth, my dearest! I am playing a role and it requires a uniform.

LILY. I am so happy to see you! Even in this unbecoming outfit!

JACK. Unbecoming? Don't I look like an officer to you?

LILY. Not at all! *(laughs)* You appear as a comic actor at the vaudeville theatre!

JACK. *(weakly)* Yes…I suppose I do.

LILY. But we had best be wary. I am supposed to meet my aunt here and if she should see you and guess your identity –

JACK. But I have just been speaking to her!

LILY. What? All is lost then!

JACK. Quite the opposite. I dressed as a captain and came here specifically to run into the old crone. I then introduced myself to her as Captain John Staunch! *(They both laugh.)*

LILY. My darling, mischievous Jonathan! It is too delightful for words! But what are we to do next?

JACK. Don't you see? With your aunt thinking I am John Staunch we will be able to meet as often as we like and makes plans for our elopement!

LILY. You mean I must pretend that you are that awful captain?

JACK. Exactly! A little trickery and then soon comes true love!

LILY. But Jonathan, I don't know if I am capable of such a conspiracy.

JACK. Not a conspiracy, a subterfuge! After all, pretending to be in love is the next best thing to the real article.

LILY. But even pretending to love Captain John Staunch! The very idea of it fills me with repulsion!

JACK. But you've never even seen the man. He might be a very likable sort of fellow.

LILY. How can you say that, Jonathan? I shall never look at any other man but you!

JACK. Of course, my darling, that goes without saying. But if you imagine me when you must speak of him the deception will be so much easier.

LILY. I suppose that might work. I can pretend to love him but it won't seem like pretend because I'm thinking of you and not pretending at all!

JACK. Something like that.

LILY. I just hope I can pull it off.

JACK. I believe you capable of anything!

LILY. Oh, goodness! My aunt is coming this way! Well, here goes nothing!

JACK. Just remember to call me John, not Jonathan.

LILY. But that old man is with her! The father of the real John Staunch!

JACK. I forgot about father! This will never do! Come with me quick!

LILY. But I thought – !

JACK. This way! I think we'd better rehearse a bit before the performance!

(**JACK** *and* **LILY** *exit one side while* **STAUNCH** *and* **MRS. MALAPROP** *re-enter from the other side.*)

STAUNCH. Where are they going?

MALAPROP. Look how she stays so close to your son. I believe he has begun to hypothesize her already!

STAUNCH. I knew he would be crazy about her! He is my son after all!

MALAPROP. Mr. Staunch, I think Jonathan Pippin is soon going to be hoisted on his own placard.

STAUNCH. I believe you are correct again, Mrs. Malaprop. Let us return to the shop together. We still haven't tried the strawberry-flavored taffy.

MALAPROP. Oh, Mr. Staunch, you are leading me down the road of extraction!

(STAUNCH *and* MALAPROP *exit as* LOUISE *and* WILLY *enter together.*)

WILLY. Gads and geldings! I cannot believe it! After I've come all this way, left the farm, dressed up in these itchy duds, put up with the salty sea air – ! All to find out the girl is spoken for!

LOUISE. I'm afraid it's all true, Mr. Furrow. Miss Lily is intended for –

WILLY. Don't even utter the rogue's name! I couldn't bear to hear that he is some wealthy city slicker or one of them hoity-toity types from Long Island! Oh, dobbins and donkeys!! Who is it, Louise? Might as well drop the whole bale of hay on me!

LOUISE. Well, he is a man of some money. He is –

WILLY. How could she tumble to such a man! The girl sat on that horse like she was born to it! She belongs on the farm!

LOUISE. I'm afraid her intended is a city feller all right. His name is –

WILLY. Oh, if only my friend Jack was here! He'd tell me what to do.

LOUISE. Jack?

WILLY. Captain John Staunch. And a damn fine fellow he is too! He'd know what I oughta do. He's a college boy, you see.

LOUISE. The Captain is a friend of yours?

WILLY. Close as they come. I'd trust him with my finest Tennessee Walker in a hailstorm. But he's got his own life to live, I reckon. So tell me, Louise: who is my rival?

LOUISE. Well...

WILLY. Come out with it! If you want the corn to grow you got to smell the manure.

LOUISE. His name is Pippin. Jonathan Pippin!

WILLY. Pippin? What kind of name is that?

LOUISE. French, I think. He's a poet and –

WILLY. Bridles and broncos! Them girls always goes for the fancy types! What's an honest farm boy to do?

(**SHAMUS** *enters and joins them.*)

SHAMUS. There's my darlin' Louise!

LOUISE. Mr. O'Slugger! Do you have that new love letter ready for Delilah?

SHAMUS. Indeed I do! And a pretty piece of prose it is too!

WILLY. Don't waste you time, buddy. It's poetry the girls want these days!

SHAMUS. I don't believe I've had the pleasure, Mr…. ?

WILLY. Furrow's the name and horse raising is my game. So I'd best quit this salt water sand trap and get back to the farm where I belong.

SHAMUS. Louise, your friend seems a bit despondent. *(to* **WILLY***)* Chin up and on your toes, my friend. Life is a timed match and one cannot be caught off balance.

WILLY. What's that?

LOUISE. Mr. Furrow, this is Shamus O'Slugger, the prize fighter from Ireland that the folks are all talkin' about.

WILLY. Fighter, huh? Wrestling or fisticuffs?

SHAMUS. Boxing, Mr. Furrow! The gentlemanly art of gamesmanship that depends on a quick eye, refined footwork and a rapid left hook!

WILLY. Well, I'm impressed, Mr. O'Slugger! *(shakes hands)* Pleased to meet you. I always thought a good tug in the ring was the next best thing to a one-mile trotter's sprint.

LOUISE. Mr. Furrow is down in the dumps because he's lost his sweetheart.

SHAMUS. Lost her! In the ocean, was it?

WILLY. No, I'm the one that's all wet. Some chap from the city has stolen her heart away.

SHAMUS. It's an outrage!

LOUISE. It sure is. But I got to be getting back to the hotel. You got that letter, Mr. O'Slugger?

SHAMUS. Here it is, Louise. *(gives her the letter)* And this as well. *(gives her a coin)*

LOUISE. Why, thank you, Mr. O'Slugger! But you still owe me some more –

SHAMUS. I have not forgotten, my darlin' girl! *(blows a kiss to her)* Later. Off you go now.

LOUISE. Yes, sir! *(exits)*

SHAMUS. Tell me one thing, Mr. Furrow. Has this rival taken your place unfairly?

WILLY. If he took her fair and square I wouldn't squawk so. But the varmint used poetry and other such hocus-pocus to win her heart!

SHAMUS. Then you know what is to be done, don't you?

WILLY. Go back to Pricklepear Farm and soak my feet, I suppose.

SHAMUS. Nonsense! You must challenge the rascal to a fight!

WILLY. You mean like a duel? Oh, that's only in books and stuff.

SHAMUS. No dueling pistols or rapiers. A good honest boxing match!

WILLY. But I don't know the first thing about it. With them stuffed gloves on I'd knock myself out by wiping my brow!

SHAMUS. Don't you know, my friend, that you are speaking to an expert! And I say you have the makings of a prize fighter in you, Mr. Furrow!

WILLY. Call me Willy, please. What! Me? A boxer?

SHAMUS. Given the proper provocation and enough anger in your heart, any man can catch fire and turn the boxing ring into his personal battleground!

WILLY. You don't say…?

(The two continue to speak in pantomime as **JACK** *and* **LILY** *enter and go to another part of the stage.)*

JACK. Just try to keep your wits about you, Lily, and remember what we practiced.

LILY. Oh, Jonathan! I am so scared. And excited!

JACK. That's my girl.

SHAMUS. Remember to always come out fighting. When I'm finished training you. my lad, you'll give him such a shellacking that he'll be seeing stars!

WILLY. As you say, Mr. O'Slugger. Just as you say. Now which one is my right again?

*(***JULIE*** and ***FARLEY*** appear on opposite sides of the stage and speak to themselves.)*

JULIE. The man's so conceited, I could scream! Yet he can be such a dear…

FARLEY. I know she's far from perfect but what then am I? Oh, if only I could win her back!

*(***MALAPROP*** and ***STAUNCH*** enter together and converse without seeing the others.)*

STAUNCH. These young folks have no idea what they're talking about. Wet behind the ears! If only they would listen to the older generation!

MALAPROP. My sediments exactly, Mr. Staunch. Good old age and experience must prevail. Otherwise the world will be nothing but incontinence.

*(***LOUISE*** enters and looks at the various groups and then addresses the audience.)*

LOUISE. Well, I'd say things are in a pretty pickle. You got lovers and parents and fighters and fools…and all of them want to win the blue ribbon. Of course they all can't go home with the trophy. But ain't it sort of nice to see them all think they can? Let's let them all stew a bit while we take a break. I may be a Cupid but it ain't my wings that are sore. It's my feet.

End of Act One

ACT TWO

(LOUISE, WILLY and SHAMUS enter. WILLY is wearing boxing gloves and LOUISE carries a pencil and letter paper.)

WILLY. Lead me to the slippery upstart! *(shadow boxes)*

SHAMUS. Keep up your left, Willy! Never forget the left!

WILLY. The left! Which one is that? Oh, hang it, I'll keep up both the right and the left! That'll show him!

SHAMUS. Stay light on the feet, my friend. If both heels are on the ground you'll not have the proper balance!

WILLY. The heels can go to blazes! I'll float in the air if I got to!

LOUISE. My, Mr. Furrow, you are a sight to be scared of, that's for sure.

WILLY. Do you really think so, Louise?

LOUISE. Wait till Jonathan Pippin gets a peek at you!

WILLY. There will be blood spilt! And, bridles and broncos, it won't be mine!

SHAMUS. Himself's in a passion now! That's the spirit!

LOUISE. But ain't there a proper way to go about this sort of thing?

WILLY. Nothin' proper about a little bloodshed!

SHAMUS. Louise is right, Willy. We must present the infidel with a challenge first. Then destroy him!

WILLY. I'll challenge the fellow! *(shouts)* Jonathan Pippin, come out and fight like a man!

LOUISE. Not like that! You gotta put it in writing.

SHAMUS. Ay! Write the bloke a letter challenging him to a match and Louise here will deliver it!

WILLY. I'll do it! And they'll be fightin' words, I promise you! Give me paper!

LOUISE. You can't write nothin' with those gloves on. You and Mr. O'Slugger tell me what to write and I'll put it all down here. *(sits on bench)*

SHAMUS. That's the ticket!

WILLY. I am goin' to send such a challenge! Write this down and don't you change one phrase. "My good fellow, although you don't know me…" *(He trails off with uncertainty.)*

SHAMUS. That's no way to begin a challenge! You've got to offend the blighter! You're not asking him out to tea. This is a duel to the end!

WILLY. Yes, you're right, I must not be civil. Louise, write this down. "Dear sir, we must meet soon, don't you think? If you would be so kind as to name the place – "

SHAMUS. What's all this "dear sir" and "be so kind"? Steel yourself, call him to arms, insult his honor, let him know you're out for blood! Try again.

WILLY. "Listen to me, you no good rascal! Don't think you can steal my love from me! I don't put up with no snake in the grass! We must meet and it ain't to drink tea! I challenge you…to a fight – !" *(loses his courage)* Oh me…Oh my…

LOUISE. *(stops writing)* But don't this sound like the fight of the century. Willy the Brave versus Pippin the Knave!

SHAMUS. Keep up your anger, lad. Think of the Furrow family pride!

*(**LOUISE** continues writing.)*

WILLY. "So, you varmint, I choose the weapon and I say the boxing ring suits me! So best put up your dukes and meet me at eight o'clock tonight on the Boardwalk next to the pickle booth!"

LOUISE. That's no place to settle this matter! Make it nine o'clock under the Boardwalk near Keeney's Saloon!

SHAMUS. That's perfect!

WILLY. If you think so…

LOUISE. *(finishing writing)* "…near Keeney's Saloon." Now you sign this, Mr. Furrow.

*(**WILLY** signs the letter.)*

SHAMUS. That ought to do the trick. Off you go, Louise! *(gives her a coin)* This is for you and –

LOUISE. I know. The rest of the kisses come later. Good day, gents! *(exits with the letter)*

SHAMUS. And you come with me, Willy, my boy. We have some final preparations to make.

WILLY. More sparring practice?

SHAMUS. No. Some liquid fortification at that saloon over there. We've got the devil raging in you now but I think a dram or two is needed to keep the fellow there!

*(**WILLY** and **SHAMUS** exit in one direction as **MRS. MALAPROP** enters alone.)*

MALAPROP. I am somewhat encouraged by the prognosis that Captain Staunch has made with my niece. She never spoke once of this Jonathan Pippin creature at dinner and the girl seems more favorably incinerated when the name of John Staunch comes up. Oh, it will be such a relief to my constellation to have her wisely wed and provided for. Then I can better peruse romantic affairs of my own. I am making a refraction, of course, to Mr. Shamus O'Slugger, the man who has quite catapulted my heart.

*(**LILY** enters.)*

My niece, you are here on time! Seven o'clock exactly. I am so pleased to see you realize the importance of punctuation

LILY. I have come as you requested.

MALAPROP. I believe your meeting Captain Staunch this afternoon has had a commensurable effect on you. Is he not a fine model of a man?

LILY. I suppose he is. But Jonathan Pippin is a finer specimen all around.

MALAPROP. Again with the Jonathan Pippin! I had hoped the dashing captain had put that rudimentary right out of your head.

LILY. Mr. Pippin is also dashing. Just as dashing. More so even!

MALAPROP. I say there is no comparison at all. The captain strikes me as a man of infinitesimal behavior and proper breeding. You must admit he has subliminal manners.

LILY. Jonathan Pippin's manners are also very proper. Even more so!

MALAPROP. How could the brute have proper manners when he has never presented himself to me as a prospector should? No, again there is no comparison.

LILY. When you finally meet Mr. Pippin you will find him very much like Captain Staunch in both manners and breeding.

MALAPROP. There is no reason for me to meet the rapskeleton! Nor for you to ever see him again. Mr. Staunch and his son are due to meet us here at any moment and I believe he is going to pop the question, as the expletive goes.

LILY. The captain? Coming here? *(aside)* Now she will discover the truth!

MALAPROP. Yes. And I want you to be civil to the gentleman. No talk of this Pippin scoundrel and no matter what the captain asks you, say yes!

LILY. *(aside)* When she sees that it is not the same captain from this afternoon our charade will be destroyed! Oh, I dread meeting this horrid Captain Staunch! How I wish my Jonathan was here!

MALAPROP. What are you mumbling there? Men do not like girls that mumble. It puts them in mind of their fathers.

LILY. I was as gracious as I could be to John Staunch this afternoon but I cannot forget my Jonathan! I refuse to even look at the captain when he comes. It is more than I can bear! *(sits on a bench facing out)*

MALAPROP. You stubborn girl! You will look at him and you will say yes when he proposes to you and the matter will be settled for all indemnity!

*(**STAUNCH** enters.)*

STAUNCH. Good evening, ladies! I trust you are both well?

MALAPROP. Mr. Staunch! We are as well as nature and our temperature allows. But where is your son?

STAUNCH. Coming directly, Mrs. Malaprop. He wanted to stop at that flower shop over there and get Miss Fletcher some daisies. He is a sentimental boy at heart.

MALAPROP. He is that indeed. Sentiment flows in the man like fruits and vegetables from a coronary!

LILY. *(aside)* He sounds more awful by the minute!

*(**JACK** enters, still in uniform, and carrying a bouquet of flowers which he uses to hide his face when he must get close to **LILY**.)*

STAUNCH. Ah! Here he is now!

LILY. *(aside)* Now it comes!

MALAPROP. My dear Captain Staunch! *(takes his hand)* Your arrival is most proportional. My niece and I have been anxiously waiting for you.

LILY. *(aside)* Is she so blind that she doesn't notice it's not the same man?

JACK. *(speaking in a nasal or other odd voice)* So charmed to make your acquaintance. Again, that is!

STAUNCH. What's the matter with the boy?

MALAPROP. I hope you have not caught a cold, Captain. There is so much introspection going around these days.

JACK. *(even more nasal)* Not at all, Mrs. Malaprop. I believe the salmon I had at dinner has scratched my throat.

LILY. *(aside)* Such a horrid sounding man! I cannot bring myself to look at him!

MALAPROP. Well, do not waste your words on myself, Captain. There is someone sitting over there who would much rather you speak to her.

STAUNCH. Woo her, Jack! Damn the salmon and full speed ahead!

JACK. Of course.

(**JACK** *carefully approaches* **LILY** *on the bench and speaks to her in his odd, unappealing voice. He hides somewhat behind the flowers and she refuses to look directly at him so their eyes never meet until the end of his speech.*)

My dear Miss Fletcher…I…I know that you do not know me well…not at all, actually. But my intentions are sincere. You must believe that. And although it is not an easy thing for you to do, I ask that you open up your heart to me. I feel like a man in disguise but I am sure that if you would just look into my eyes you will discover that…that I love you.

(*During the last lines his voice has returned to normal and there is sincerity in his tone. On his last word* **LILY** *finally looks at him, he takes the flowers from his face and presents them to her. She sees it is* **JACK.***)

LILY. Jonathan!

STAUNCH. Jonathan? What the devil does the girl mean? That's my son Jack!

LILY. My Jonathan!

MALAPROP. Her head is so full of that antediluvian artist that she sees him everywhere. Apologize at once to Captain Staunch!

LILY. But this is my Jonathan!

STAUNCH. The girl is loony! Jack, will you settle for a loony bride?

MALAPROP. What is the matter with the little husky?

JACK. I fear Miss Fletcher is quite right in the head.

LILY. Jonathan, tell them who you are! Surely the captain's father must realize you are not his son.

STAUNCH. Not my son? She's gone bughouse!

MALAPROP. I fear the sun has perspirated her parasol and gone directly into her brain!

JACK. The time has come for me to confess the truth to everyone. Miss Fletcher, I am indeed John Staunch. Mrs. Malaprop, I am also Jonathan Pippin. Father, I am a deceiving son who has played falsely with everyone here.

STAUNCH. So you…! You, the penniless artist? Your own rival? *(laughs)* My son, you're not such a dull and dimwitted boy as I imagined! You mischievous scamp, you! Your own rival! And pretending not to be infatuated with this lovely child here! Just going to marry her to please me! Ha! That's a good one, my boy! *(continues laughing)*

JACK. I fear that the two ladies are not as amused as you, father. I have used them wrongly and deceived them beyond humor.

STAUNCH. *(stops laughing)* Oh. You might be right there, Jack.

MALAPROP. You disseminating villain!

STAUNCH. Yep. It looks like you're right, Jack.

MALAPROP. Then it was you who wrote that letter! It was you that reflected on my parts of speech!

JACK. I must admit I was the author, Mrs. Malaprop. But at the time I was not fully acquainted with the real Mrs. Malaprop.

MALAPROP. It is too late for flattery, young man! I have been wounded to morality! In fact, I am so humiliated that I do not think I can stand here before you without being overcome with a nervous probate! *(exits)*

STAUNCH. But it has all worked out as we planned, Mrs. Malaprop –! Oh, dear. Maybe I had better talk to her. Everything will be fine, I promise you two lovebirds. Mrs. Malaprop – ! *(exits)*

JACK. You have said nothing, Miss Fletcher.

LILY. What is there to say, Captain Staunch? It seems I am engaged to marry you whether I like or not. So nothing I say will matter –

JACK. Please forgive me, Lily! I had my reasons!

LILY. When we played at trickery, I didn't think that I was the one being deceived.

JACK. I thought you would not fall in love with John Staunch so –

LILY. Oh, I understand. Well, I shall marry you, Captain Staunch. And I will be a good wife to you. But I will always miss Jonathan Pippin, the one true love of my life.

(She runs off. **JACK** *starts after her but* **LOUISE** *enters from the opposite side and calls him back.)*

LOUISE. Captain Staunch! Or is it Mr. Pippin I'm talking to now?

JACK. It no longer makes any difference, Louise. They are one and the same.

LOUISE. Well, that makes this easier to deliver. *(gives him the letter)*

JACK. What is it? From Lily? *(He reads it quickly.)*

LOUISE. Not quite. It's the Irish boxer that put him up to it. He got Mr. Furrow all riled up and taught him how to box and – !

JACK. Why, it's from Willy! What does he mean that I stole his love away from him?

LOUISE. It's Miss Lily! He kinda took a shine to her.

JACK. Well, the way Miss Fletcher feels about me right now, she might prefer honest Willy. I will meet him as it says here and try to settle the whole mess. Meanwhile, I must see Lily and beg her forgiveness.

*(***LOUISE*** exits one direction and* **JACK** *starts out the other way but he runs into* **SHAMUS** *who is a bit drunk.)*

SHAMUS. Excuse me, sir! I have words to say to you and they are mighty words so I suggest you weigh them carefully!

JACK. I beg your pardon, my good sir, but I do not know you. I am afraid that in your inebriated state you have mistaken me for someone else.

SHAMUS. I have mistaken no one! I know you by sight, if not by name! It is the uniform that gives you away, sir.

JACK. I have no quarrel with you so good day and farewell. *(tries to exit)*

SHAMUS. But I have a quarrel with you, sir! Were you not on the Boardwalk this afternoon with a darlin' little gal dressed all in yellow? The two of you were walking together and you seemed to show a rather intimate sort of friendliness to the beauty.

JACK. It is no business of yours, sir, who I walked with and where!

SHAMUS. Oh, but it is my business! No one gets intimate with my little Delilah when she has given her heart to me!

JACK. Delilah? But the young lady who was with me –

SHAMUS. So you cannot deny it! I demand retribution, sir. You will meet me at your earliest convenience and I will defend the honor of my Delilah in a boxing match.

JACK. Another boxing match?

SHAMUS. At your earliest convenience or I will call forth your cowardice!

JACK. This is absurd! My earliest convenience… *(looks at the letter)* How about tonight at nine o'clock under the Boardwalk near Keeney's Saloon?

SHAMUS. It is done! I will see you there. By the way, my name is Shamus O'Slugger and I will provide the boxing gloves.

JACK. You are too kind.

SHAMUS. Think nothing of it. *(burps)* Until later, sir.

JACK. Yes. I wouldn't miss it for the world. *(exits)*

SHAMUS. Keeney's Saloon…Nine o'clock…Well, that's damn convenient, I'm sure!

*(He staggers off as **JULIE** enters.)*

JULIE. What a silly girl I have become! I've been walking up and down this Boardwalk for an hour now. Half of the time I'm hoping I'll run into Farley, the rest of the time I'm trying to avoid seeing him again! I was not like this before. I was always a sensible girl; it was Farley who was moody and indecisive and – so foolish in his love. I think that's what I so admired in him. But now –

(FARLEY enters. Both see each other and stop. Then FARLEY goes to her.)

FARLEY. Miss Whitaker...

JULIE. Mr. Danes...

FARLEY. It will be dark soon.

JULIE. Yes. There's a bit of moon over there. Very thin and frail looking.

FARLEY. Hardly a moon at all really.

JULIE. Perhaps you could write a poem about it, Mr. Danes. Isn't that what poets do when they see something of interest?

FARLEY. Some poets. I would probably brood about why it's so thin and how much I'd prefer it be a full moon. I am such a ridiculous fellow.

JULIE. I must admit that sometimes I do like your brooding so, Mr. Danes. It makes you so attractive.

FARLEY. You did not think so this afternoon, Miss Whitaker.

JULIE. No. I was a bit harsh with you. I thought your brooding over me was a sign of mistrust. I see now that if such was the case, you would mistrust the moon itself.

FARLEY. Can you ever forgive me, Julie?

JULIE. Oh, I suppose I already have. After our quarrel this afternoon, when I walked away from you, I soon realized that I was walking away from the person who meant more to me than any other.

FARLEY. Oh, Julie, I've been such a fool!

JULIE. Of course, my dear. What else can one expect?

FARLEY. When I thought I had lost you, I realized for the first time the true depths of despair. It was not posing or moody or even poetic. It was sincere sorrow. Julie, I don't need to write verses any more. My love for you is all the poetry I shall ever need.

(He kisses her as **LILY** *enters alone.)*

LILY. Dear Julie, I see you have found Mr. Danes after all.

JULIE. Yes, Lily. And to think I had almost lost him forever!

FARLEY. Good evening, Miss Fletcher.

LILY. I fear it is not, Mr. Danes. I have had an unpleasant revelation tonight. Something that I fear will not come as a surprise to you.

FARLEY. Does it concern Jack?

LILY. Jack indeed. For that's who my beloved Jonathan Pippin has turned out to be.

FARLEY. I confess I knew of the deception and several times warned Jack that no good would come of it. So he has finally told you the truth?

LILY. He was found out. The joke came to an end and I was betrothed to a stranger.

JULIE. My poor Lily! To be deceived like that! Do you still wish to marry Mr. Pippin – I mean, Captain Staunch?

LILY. I am so confused, Julie. Jonathan was everything I ever dreamed of in a man! Our love was secret and passionate and both of us were willing to risk every-thing for happiness. But now that he is John Staunch, and approved of by my aunt and everything is agreed on…well, it's not the same kind of love.

JULIE. Perhaps it is a more realistic kind of love. The kind that does not need secrets and elopement and such.

LILY. Oh, do you think so, Julie?

*(**LOUISE** rushes on.)*

LOUISE. Miss Lily! There you are at last! And Mr. Danes and Miss Julie too! Oh, what's gonna happen!

LILY. What is it, Louise?

LOUISE. It's Shamus. I mean, Mr. O'Slugger!

FARLEY. That boxing champion who's in town?

LOUISE. That's the one! He's challenged Mr. Pippin to a match! I mean, he's gonna fight Captain Staunch!

LILY. Whatever for?

LOUISE. It don't matter the reason! But the poor captain is gonna get hurt real bad, I just know it!

FARLEY. She's right. O'Slugger has been known to cripple his opponents in the ring. Especially if his anger is aroused!

(STAUNCH *and* MALAPROP *enter.*)

MALAPROP. Lily! Oh, Lily! The most terrible thing has happened!

LILY. I've just heard about Captain Staunch and that Irish boxer.

MALAPROP. Yes! The dear boy is in unsaturated danger!

LILY. But I thought you were very displeased with the captain for deceiving you, Aunt.

STAUNCH. Oh, that's all been cleared up. Jack didn't mean anything by it. Although I will admit he went a bit too far in that letter.

MALAPROP. Time is very crucible! We must find out where this boxing match is to be held and stop it!

LOUISE. I know where! Under the boardwalk near Keeney's Saloon at nine o'clock!

STAUNCH. Nine o'clock! We haven't much time!

FARLEY. I think I know where Keeney's is. Come along with me!

LILY. Quickly, Mr. Danes!

MALAPROP. We must prevent this calligraphy!

(*All rush off. The lighting changes and* WILLY *and* SHAMUS *enter, both a bit drunk.* WILLY *wears boxing gloves and* SHAMUS *carries a second pair.*)

WILLY. Gads and geldings! I hope this fellow Pippin has no more experience with these durned things than me! They are the most awkward mittens a fellow can come up against.

SHAMUS. Even if the rogue is a champion of the ring, you have the advantage of knowing your reasons are just!

WILLY. A champion! You don't think so, do you Shamus?

SHAMUS. His wrongdoing has fired up your blood. He does not share that advantage.

WILLY. Fire in my blood! Of course! That's what I got! All the same, it would be better if he's never boxed before in his life.

SHAMUS. Regardless of his experience, he'll not soon forget this day.

WILLY. I'm a little afeared that neither will I. Now which is my left again…?

SHAMUS. Here he comes now!

WILLY. *(turns his back)* I can't bear to look! What if he has fire in his blood too?

SHAMUS. The shameful womanizer approaches!

WILLY. Is he a big fellow, Shamus? Say he is small and sickly looking. Maybe with a peg leg?

SHAMUS. He seems fit enough. By Jesu, I recognize the cur now! He is the very man who displayed such attention to my Delilah! The knave's appetite is insatiable!

WILLY. Oh, that sounds bad!

(**JACK** *enters.*)

SHAMUS. You are Jonathan Pippin, sir?

JACK. I will answer to any of his debts or actions.

SHAMUS. Then you have two quarrels to answer tonight. First you have stolen the heart of the beloved object of affection of this honest farmer here and, secondly, you have behaved in a shocking manner with my delicate mistress Delilah! Which will you answer to first?

JACK. How about both at once?

SHAMUS. What!

WILLY. Oh, that sounds like a good idea, Shamus! Then you can do the bulk of the boxing and I'll provide the fire in my blood for encouragement.

SHAMUS. *(to* **JACK***)* You are cocky, sir. I am not amused by your suggestion.

WILLY. It seems like a good suggestion, though. *(turns to face* **JACK***)* Sir, if you wouldn't mind – Jack!

JACK. Good evening, Willy.

WILLY. What are you doing here?

JACK. I have come in answer to your letter. I am…or rather, I was…Jonathan Pippin.

WILLY. How can you be this Pippin when everyone knows you're Jack Staunch?

JACK. It was a ruse that failed badly. But everybody knows my true name now.

SHAMUS. Pippin or Staunch or whatever, there is a matter of business to be settled here, sir. Willy, prepare yourself!

WILLY. Fight Jack? I can't do that. He's a pal of mine!

SHAMUS. A pal who stole the love of your life away from you.

WILLY. Oh. That. Jack, why didn't you tell me it was Lily you was sweet on?

JACK. Why didn't you say that Miss Fletcher was the filly you were after?

WILLY. I guess it never came up. We have so many more interesting things to chat about than women.

SHAMUS. *(to* **WILLY***)* Are you saying you will not defend your right to the lady?

WILLY. Well…I did like the way she rode side saddle. She looked like a queen up on that horse! But it was Jack who sent her to me for ridin' lessons so I guess I sorta took her away from him.

JACK. And perhaps you can have her still, Willy. Miss Fletcher is quite angry with me at the moment – and with good cause, I might add – so she might yet be yours.

SHAMUS. Mother of God! This is the most shameful exchange of politeness I have ever seen! Stop offering the girl to each other and put up your dukes!

WILLY. But do you think Lily would be happy at Pricklepear Farm? She seems more the city type.

JACK. Perhaps she would be happier with an honest man who has not deceived her.

WILLY. Oh, Jack! Don't be so hard on yourself!

SHAMUS. You're both disgusting cowards, I tell you!

JACK. But I do love her, Willy. I was so afraid of losing her that I made up Jonathan Pippin in the first place. But I've hurt her dearly and now must pay the price.

WILLY. Oh, Jack, I'm sure she'll forgive you. Let me talk to the girl –

SHAMUS. Enough of this! *(to* **JACK***)* Sir, you still have to answer to me. And you will find I am not such a weak-willed fool as this farmer here.

WILLY. Well, I like that! Shamus, you've gotta learn to calm down and relax a little.

SHAMUS. *(to* **JACK***)* Sir, I also have fire in my blood and it will not be satisfied with pleasant talk! Prepare to fight for the honor of my beloved Delilah!

JACK. As you wish, my hot-blooded fellow. I have never seen this Delilah but she sounds like a splendid girl so I'll battle for her good name.

(**WILLY** *helps put the gloves on* **JACK.***)*

SHAMUS. Never heard of her indeed! Myself spied the two of you whispering together this afternoon on the Boardwalk! I will not stand for that kind of friendliness with my fiancee!

WILLY. Now you be careful, Jack. This fellow has more ribbons and trophies than a prize thoroughbred after Derby season.

JACK. I never went in for boxing except a little at college but I shouldn't make too much a fool of myself.

WILLY. And watch his left hook. He tells me it's something fearful!

SHAMUS. Are you ready, sir?

JACK. At your pleasure. But be wary of my anger, sir. It grows more and more in your presence.

(They start boxing. **SHAMUS** *is a bit more surefooted but* **JACK** *holds his own.)*

WILLY. That a way, Jack! Keep your left up! Watch the right foot – it's falling back too much!

JACK. Where did you learn so much about boxing, Willy?

SHAMUS. From a master. I suggest you heed his instructions! *(gives* **JACK** *a hard punch)*

WILLY. Oh, Jack! Didn't I tell you about his left hook? It's the talk of Ireland, they say.

JACK. I well believe it! *(swings at* **SHAMUS** *but misses)*

WILLY. Watch your foot work, Jack! He's dancin' round you like some kinda horsefly!

SHAMUS. This is for my Delilah!

*(***SHAMUS** *punches* **JACK** *twice and he falls to the ground as* **LILY, FARLEY, JULIE, STAUNCH, MALAPROP** *and* **LOUISE** *rush on.)*

LILY. Jack!

STAUNCH. There they are!

JACK. Did she call me Jack?

WILLY. Sure sounds like it.

MALAPROP. Stop this alteration immediately!

STAUNCH. You heard the lady. Stop, at once!

LILY. *(rushing to* **JACK***)* Oh, my dearest! You're bleeding!

JACK. Lily? Is it really you?

SHAMUS. Take no sympathy on him, Delilah. The rogue deserves none of your tears.

LILY. *(to SHAMUS)* Shut up, you bully!

FARLEY. Are you all right, Jack?

STAUNCH. Speak to me, son! Say you're not dead!

JACK. No, father. But I am in a sorry state.

MALAPROP. Look at the poor boy. Beaten to a pulpit! You ought to be ashamed of yourself, Mr. O'Slugger! I am quite indentured to change my opinion of you, sir.

LILY. Oh, Jack! For your name is Jack and not Jonathan.

JACK. Even though you wish it were the other way around.

LILY. Not any longer, my dearest. I will be pleased to be Mrs. John Staunch.

JACK. Oh, Lily! *(They embrace.)*

SHAMUS. Delilah! What is meant by this shameful exhibition?

LILY. Are you addressing me, you brute?

SHAMUS. Don't you recognize your own name? And what's he doing calling you Lily?

LILY. I fear you have been deceived, sir, if you think I am called Delilah. I know no one of that name.

SHAMUS. What's this?

LOUISE. There is no real Delilah. It was only a pen name, Mr. O'Slugger. A non da plum used by a certain lady who took a likin' to you.

LILY. But I was not that lady.

SHAMUS. Then who was she?

MALAPROP. Quagmire no further, my dear Shamus! I am the lady in question!

SHAMUS. Yourself, is it? By all the saints, I have been used poorly!

MALAPROP. Not by me, Shamus. I was always the pomegranate of faithfulness.

SHAMUS. I beg your pardon, madam. But I'm thinking that I am greatly disappointed. *(to* **JACK***)* I concede the boxing match, sir, and give you the prize of Delilah!

MALAPROP. You rude Irish tripod! I expected more from a gentleman from Hibernation!

SHAMUS. To listen to you, madam, I believe without a doubt that you are the author of those letters. But someone else is responsible for this deception, I think.

LOUISE. I never said Miss Lily was Delilah! You just put two and two together and ended up love sick over the wrong girl!

SHAMUS. And all those kisses I gave you?

LOUISE. I thought they might better be spent on me than on my employer, Mrs. Malaprop.

SHAMUS. You are correct there, Louise my girl. *(laughs)* In some ways you were always my Delilah!

MALAPROP. What!

SHAMUS. And I believe I still owe you some two dozen more kisses, do I not?

LOUISE. Twenty eight, goin' by my account book.

SHAMUS. Well, keep counting, my darling girl. *(kisses her)* I will make good my promise if you will have me.

LOUISE. You big hunk of Irish stew! Of course I will! *(They kiss.)*

MALAPROP. *(weeping)* I feel completely stipulated by these events!

STAUNCH. Take heart, Mrs. Malaprop. You are too splendid a woman to be confined to a boxing ring. I've half a mind to marry you myself, madam, and spend the rest of my days just trying to figure out what you're talking about.

MALAPROP. Mr. Staunch, you are just saying that to be propagational!

STAUNCH. No, I think I'm saying it to be honest with myself. Mrs. Malaprop, will you make an old man very happy and consent to marry me?

MALAPROP. Not so old, Mr. Staunch. But oversaturated with maturity! My own! *(They embrace.)*

WILLY. There must be somethin' in this sea air after all! I haven't seen coupling like this since that spring when the new bullock – !

JACK. Pray, don't continue, Willy. We get the idea.

WILLY. Wow! This Boardwalk is really somethin'!

LOUISE. That's the truth, Mr. Furrow.

*(All freeze in position and **LOUISE** steps down to address the audience one last time.)*

And so that's how I spent the summer of 1910. When I said earlier it was a profitable summer, I wasn't just referring to coins and crispy dollar bills. I also got me a big lug of an Irishman all of my own. And every summer, whether we're in the money or no, I always insist on a visit to Atlantic City so that the old Boardwalk can keep on workin' its magic.

*(She rejoins **SHAMUS** and the cast is left in silhouette once again.)*

End of Play

PROPERTIES PLOT

Prologue
   letter (**JACK**)
   coin (**JACK**)
   letter (**MALAPROP**)
   coin (**MALAPROP**)
   letter (**JULIE**)
   letter (**FARLEY**)
   letter (**WILLY**)
   dollar bill (**WILLY**)
   1 pair of boxing gloves (**SHAMUS**)
   letter (**SHAMUS**)
   coin (**SHAMUS**)

Act One
   book (**LILY**)
   basket with 4 books inside (**LOUISE**)
   notebook and pencil (**LOUISE**)
   letter (**LOUISE**)
   coins (**SHAMUS**)
   letter (**MALAPROP**)

Act Two
   1 pair of boxing gloves (**WILLY**)
   letter paper and pencil (**LOUISE**)
   bouquet of flowers (**JACK**)
   1 pair of boxing gloves (**SHAMUS**)

Also by
Thomas Hischak...

Cinderella, Inc.

Curst Be He That Moves My Bones

Murder by the Book

The Phony Physician

Rutherford Wolf

The Swine of Avon

Twice the Usual Number of Suspects

Willabella Witch's Last Spell

Please visit our website **bakersplays.com** for complete
descriptions and licensing information.